Table of Contents

Rourke
Educational Media
rourkeeducationalmedia.com

Can you find these words?

rain forest | skyscrapers

stilts | suburb

Where We Live

People live in many kinds of places.

Some places are hot.

People build near water to keep cool.

A rain forest is wet!

rain forest

6

stilts

A house on **stilts** stays dry.

A city is crowded. People build up!

skyscrapers

They live in **skyscrapers**.

There is more space in a **suburb**.

suburb

Houses can be large or small.

In farming areas, pigs and horses have houses too!

Did you find these words?

A **rain forest** is wet!

They live in **skyscrapers**.

A house on **stilts** stays dry.

There is more space in a **suburb**.

Photo Glossary

 **rain forest** (rayn FOR-ist): A tropical forest where a lot of rain falls much of the year.

 **skyscrapers** (SKYE-skray-purs): Very tall buildings often found in cities.

 **stilts** (stilts): Posts that hold a building above the ground or water level.

 **suburb** (SUHB-urb): An area on the outer edge of a city with mostly homes and few businesses.

Index

About the Author

Tammy Brown writes books and teaches teachers how to teach their students to read. She enjoys walking in the woods.

www.rourkeeducationalmedia.com

PHOTO CREDITS: Cover: ©tacojim; p. 2,6,14,15: ©gualtiero boffi/©Alamy Stock Photo; p. 2,8,14,15: ©SeanPavonePhoto; p: 2,10,14,15: ©IP Galanternik D.U.; p. 3: ©Alexphotographic; p. 4: ©Travel Stock; p. 12: ©alexmak7; p. 13: ©LOSHADENOK

Edited by: Keli Sipperley
Cover design by: Kathy Walsh
Interior design by: Rhea Magaro-Wallace

Library of Congress PCN Data
Where We Live / Tammy Brown
(Plants, Animals, and People)
ISBN (hard cover)(alk. paper) 978-1-64156-159-4
ISBN (soft cover) 978-1-64156-215-7
ISBN (e-Book) 978-1-64156-270-6
Library of Congress Control Number: 2017957771

Printed in the United States of America, North Mankato, Minnesota